D1405475

Dear Leah,
   thank you for reading
our story.
   REiS and Joan Kaufman
                  3/18

P.S. Keep reading!

To my directionally challenged son Brad,
who is my other favorite child

www.mascotbooks.com

Wrong Way Reis

©2018 Joan Kaufman. All Rights Reserved. No part of this publication may be reproduced, stored in a retrieval system or transmitted in any form by any means electronic, mechanical, or photocopying, recording or otherwise without the permission of the author.

For more information, please contact:
Mascot Books
620 Herndon Parkway #320
Herndon, VA 20170
info@mascotbooks.com

Library of Congress Control Number: 2017912236

CPSIA Code: PRT1017A
ISBN-13: 978-1-68401-275-6

Printed in the United States

WRONG WAY REIS

Joan Kaufman

illustrated by Joe Chouinard

Hi!
My name is
Reis

...and I want to share some very exciting news with you.

Every year, my family and I fly from New York to Florida to migrate for the winter months. Some people who do that are called "snowbirds," but my family and I are real snowbirds because we're Canadian geese!

But that's not the exciting part.

The exciting part is...

But not just any birthday. It's my 10th birthday and that means I can finally lead our flock. You see, every time we fly to Florida, a different family member heads the V formation. A V formation is the most aerodynamic way to fly (that means it's the fastest), but you have to be 10 years old to lead. Finally, it's my turn.

When the time came for us to leave, everyone got in formation behind me and we took to the skies! I waved goodbye to all of my bird friends below who weren't migrating. Boy, were they going to be cold!

I lead my flock around the Statue of Liberty and honked, "We'll be back in three months!"

I think Ms. Liberty smiled back at us!

Everything was wonderful. The weather was great and the winds were favorable underneath our wings. This leading stuff was easy! I was a natural.

About an hour later, my mother signaled that it was time to land so we could have a rest and have a snack. So I headed down from the sky with my flock following closely. But as we got lower, something wasn't right.

Could it be?

Were my eyes playing tricks on me or did that statue look familiar?

"Wrong Way Reis! Wrong Way Reis!"

my cousins chanted as we landed next to the statue again.

I hung my head low. How did I get so off-course? I wandered away from my flock, embarrassed. I was the worst leader of all time.

Mom put her wing around me. "Don't feel badly, Reis. It was your first time."

"Some birds just don't have a good sense of direction," added Dad. "When we get to Florida, we'll take you to Dr. Pelican for a check-up. Maybe she can help you with your directional problem."

"But you should probably let someone else lead the V until then," said Mom.

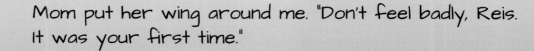

Two days later, we arrived in Florida and our first stop was the office of Dr. Pelican. After a few tests, she said, "You seem fine."

"What do you mean 'fine'?" I said. "I flew around in circles! I could've crashed us all back into Lady Liberty! You must have some medicine for me."

"I don't have any medicine," said Dr. Pelican, "but why don't you go see Herbert. He's a humpback whale who lives nearby. I visited him last year about this time of year and he seemed to have the same problem. You might find it useful to talk to him. He's right past the Bahamas, just look for all the little islands. Off you go!"

"Herbert!"

I honked, circling over the ocean. I had been at it for a while. "Herbert! Herbert!"

Finally, a giant whale surfaced and called up, "Hello, little bird! Please come land on me so we can talk."

I swooped down and landed gracefully (almost). Then I told Herbert all about my problem and how Dr. Pelican had sent me.

"I used to have the same problem," he said, "but I found a solution. It's called a GPS. That's a Global Positioning System. It talks to me and tells me which way to go when I migrate."

"Where can I find one of those?" I asked.

"The electronics store—" Herbert checked his GPS and pointed "—that way."

I flew directly to the electronics store to get my very own GPS. Well, not directly because I got lost a few times.

The sales person was very nice and attached the GPS directly to my wing. Then he set the voice to speak in Honkgarian and showed me how to enter the address of where I wanted to go. I couldn't wait to try it out!

Three months later, my aunts and uncles said they'd give me a second chance to lead the group. I stretched out my wings, plugged NYC into my GPS, then proudly took to the front of the V.

"Go up to 900 feet, then turn left for 1,000 miles," said my GPS.

"No problem!" I said right back. It was smooth sailing. Until...

"Re-routing. Turn right in 200 feet."

I must've gone off course. We can't all be perfect.

At the end of the second day of our trip, my GPS voice announced, "You have arrived at your destination."

I looked down and...

we made it!

"Good job, Reis!" everyone cheered as we landed.

"Way to go!" said my aunt as she patted my back.

All of my little cousins even asked if they could get a GPS for their wings too!

I had finally solved my problem, and I knew for sure I was headed in the right direction.

About the Author

Joan Stern Kaufman is a retired high school math teacher. She lives in Long Island, New York, with her (also directionally-challenged) husband who owns four GPS systems.

Her three grandsons, Brandon, Danny, and Eli, helped edit this book. Their input was invaluable.